Published 2005 by **Being Lotte Books Limited**
Cromwell Tower, Barbican, London EC2Y 8DD

Text and illustration copyright © Tim Epps, 2005
All rights reserved

British Library Cataloguing in Publication Data
A CIP catalogue record for this book is available
from the British Library

ISBN 0-9548122-1-2

Printed in Italy by IPF-Maniago/Pn

www.beinglotte.com

To Philomena

Being Lotte at home

Tim Epps

Being Lotte Books

Lotte is looking out of the window.

It is very wet and windy today.

Being Lotte she doesn't want to go out and get wet and blown about.

She can have a nice day staying at home instead.

Lotte can have fun finding out all about the jobs that need to be done around the house.

First, there are the breakfast things to be cleared away and washed.

Perhaps Lotte can help.

What's all this?

Being Lotte she has decided that washing the breakfast things looks like a lot of fun.

Those bubbles are for washing the plates and mugs Lotte, not you!

Lotte has gone into one of the bedrooms to see what's going on in there.

The bed is in a bit of a jumble!

It needs to be made nice and neat and tidy.

Do you think Lotte can help?

What a surprise!

Being Lotte she has jumped into the bed after helping to make it neat and tidy.

She has made herself nice and cosy hasn't she?

Perhaps she is going to have a nap!

Lotte is looking at some beautiful flowers.

They have a lovely smell.

All the flowers in the house need watering.

Do you think Lotte can help water the flowers?

Oh dear!

I don't think Lotte is very good with the watering can.

Being Lotte she has knocked some of the flowers over.

But they do make rather a fancy hat.

Very pretty, Lotte!

It is time to do the washing.

All the dirty clothes have to be collected in the basket ready to go in the washing machine.

Lotte has found a sock that was left behind.

Sploosh!

Being Lotte she has opened the washing machine to put the sock in.

All the water is pouring out!

Don't get wet feet, Lotte.

Lotte is watching while the dusting is done.

The duster's feathers are very pretty - just like the colours in a rainbow!

Perhaps Lotte is going to have a closer look.

Atchooo!

Being Lotte she has got dust up her nose.

It has made her sneeze and she has blown all the feathers off the duster.

Now it's raining feathers!

Lotte can smell something cooking.

She has found everything needed for making cakes.

Lotte looks very excited!

Do you think she will try to make a cake?

Wow!

Being Lotte she has made some delicious Lotte cookies.

They look very yummy!

How clever, Lotte.

Do you think she knows that there is flour on her nose?

Lotte got very dirty today!

She needs a good bath.

Being Lotte she loves a nice warm bubble bath.

Her little rubber duck loves it too!

It has been a very busy day for Lotte.

It is time for her to go to bed.

Being Lotte she has found a friendly teddy bear to snuggle down with.

Night-night, Lotte.

Sweet dreams.

The End

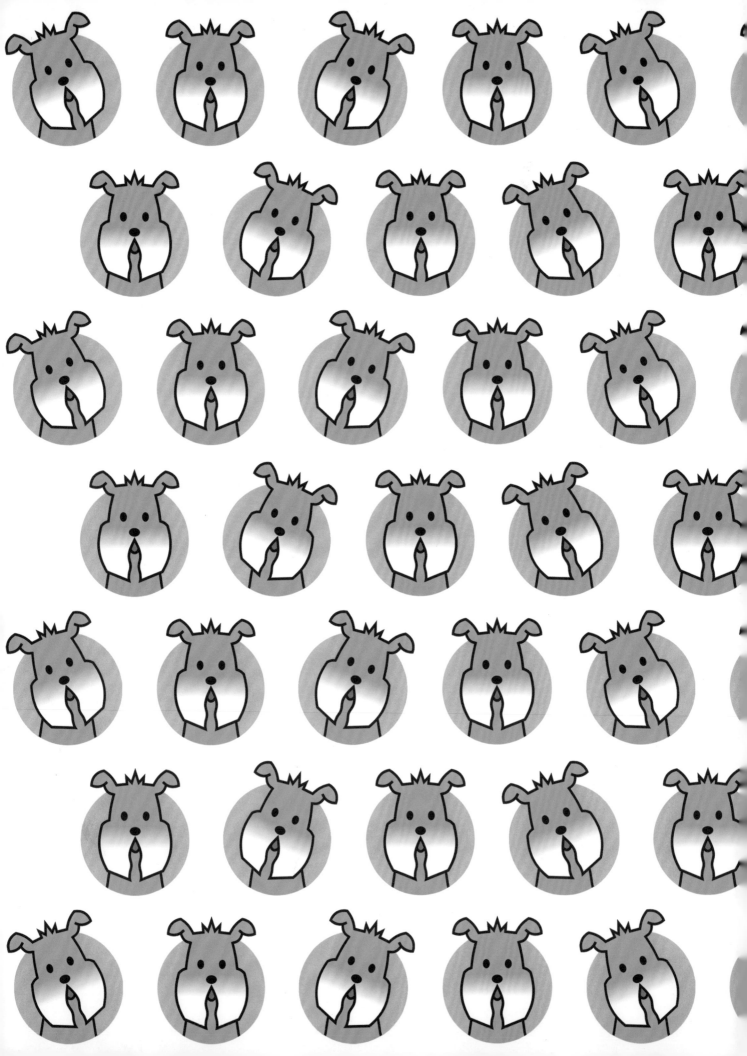